A HAPPY ENDING BOOK ™

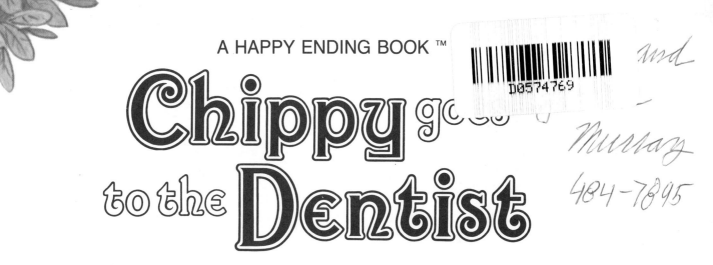

Chippy goes to the Dentist

by Jane Carruth   illustrated by Tony Hutchings

MODERN PUBLISHING
A Division of Unisystems, Inc.
New York, New York 10022

It was Chippy's birthday, and he was having a party. All
his little friends had brought him presents, and Mommy
had made a lovely big birthday cake.

After the party, Chippy began to play with one of his presents—a super toy train.

"Don't forget to brush your teeth," Mommy called from the kitchen. But Chippy pretended not to hear. He helped himself to another caramel instead!

The next morning, Chippy told his mother that he didn't want any breakfast. "I can't eat," he whispered.

"You must have a toothache," Mommy said. "Did you brush your teeth after the party?"

When Chippy didn't seem able to remember, Mommy had a look at his bad tooth. Then she said, "We must visit Doctor Nutkins, the dentist."

When Chippy's tooth stopped aching so much, he went outside to play with his friend, Susie.

"What's it like—going to the dentist?" he asked, as he climbed on the see-saw.

"I don't know," said Susie. "I've never been to one!"

Later in the morning, Susie invited Chippy to a picnic in her garden. Her mother had made delicious sandwiches and cupcakes with icing. Chippy forgot all about his tooth as he munched away at the sandwiches and cupcakes.

After the picnic, Susie told Chippy she was going to brush her teeth. "I always do," she said, "after eating sweet things."

Chippy followed her into the bathroom. But when she offered him a new toothbrush so that he could brush his teeth too, Chippy said, "No thanks! I would rather go out and play."

When Chippy got home, Mommy was waiting to take him to the dentist. "There's no need!" he cried. "My tooth doesn't ache any more!" And just to prove it, he asked for a crunchy cookie.

"If you're sure," said Mommy, "I'll finish doing the wash."

"I'm sure," smiled Chippy. And he was so happy that he ran out again and began hanging up the towels.

That night Chippy had a dream. He dreamt that lots of little tooth-men with tiny arms and legs were doing a war-dance around his head. He was so scared of their fierce, frowning faces that he began to cry.

His crying brought Mommy into his room. She held him in her arms and wiped away his tears. And when he told her about the fierce little tooth-men, she nodded her head. "I think that bad tooth of yours made you dream like that," she said. "We'll go to see Doctor Nutkins in the morning."

Chippy took firm hold of his mother's dress as they went into the dentist's waiting-room the next day. He was so scared he didn't see how friendly it looked! He just saw poor little Bushtail holding his swollen, lumpy cheek and looking miserable!

Mommy picked up a book with pretty pictures, but Chippy was too frightened to look at the pictures. He was wondering what Doctor Nutkins was doing to poor little Bushtail! He was also wondering what Doctor Nutkins would do to him!

Imagine his surprise when the door of the dentist's room burst open and out came Bushtail and his Daddy. And Bushtail was grinning cheerfully. "See you later!" he laughed.

Chippy clung on to his mother's hand as they went in to see the dentist. Doctor Nutkins smiled and told Chippy to sit in his big chair. "I don't suppose it will take very long to fill that bad tooth of yours," said Doctor Nutkins.

Chippy kept his eyes on the spinning mobile above his head while Doctor Nutkins began to drill the bad tooth.

"Dear me," said the dentist, as he worked. "I can see you haven't been brushing your teeth. You've been giving them a chance to be bad, haven't you?"

Before Chippy could think of anything to say, there was Doctor Nutkins helping him out of the big chair. "Well, that bad tooth of yours should behave itself now," said the dentist. "And here's a little present for you. Just remember to give it plenty of work to do!"

Chippy hopped and skipped all the way home because his tooth wasn't hurting any more. When he opened his present and found it was a brand-new toothbrush, he wasn't really surprised! Chippy soon forgot all about his bad tooth. But one thing he didn't forget—and that was to give his toothbrush lots of work to do every day!